NOT JUST THE DRIVER!

written by **Sara Holly Ackerman**

illustrated by **Robert Neubecker**

Beach Lane Books   New York London Toronto Sydney New Delhi

Who makes buses rev and go
through detours, gridlock, storms, and snow?
Block by block, who smooths the journey—
potholed, hilly, twisty, turn-y?

Bus mechanics peer inside
to check if you can safely ride.
Engine tune-up—zooming faster!

Brake repair—avoid disaster!
Change the spark plugs, new transmission.
VROOM away in top condition.

Who takes care of cargo loads
trucking over endless roads?

Who makes sure it's all designed
so shipments never fall behind?

In the warehouse, loaders lift,
box the goods up, stack, and shift.
Pallets, cartons, crates galore—
BEEP, BEEP, BEEP! Here come some more!
Now the big rig's full of freight
for hauling down the interstate.

Who leads subways to the station,
gliding to their destination?
Who's in charge of traffic flow
in busy tunnels down below?

IT'S NOT JUST THE OPERATOR!

Signal maintainers search for glitches,
fix the lights, replace the switches.
Different colors indicate:

"Time to go!" or "Stop and wait,"
so that they can make decisions,
steering clear of—*SCREECH!*—collisions.

Who sends riders—*CLICK, CLICK, CLACK!*—
down the proper railroad track?

Who provides them with direction,
chugging toward the right connection?

IT'S NOT JUST THE ENGINEER!

Ticket agents tell it straight:
train line, station, time, and date,
helping travelers make their way
to places where they work and play.

They send riders rushing toward the platform where it's *ALL ABOARD!*

Who guides floating fleets with ease
and water-travel expertise?
Who checks weather, minds the clock,
brings the ferry in to dock?

From an office perched on land,
calm dispatchers lend a hand,
guiding vessels back and forth,
eastward, westward, south to north.
They study routes. They double-check.
TOOT, TOOT, TOOT!—all hands on deck!

HARBORMASTER

Who moves airplanes day and night,
off the runway into flight?

Who brings airplanes to the ground,
to land and taxi safe and sound?

IT'S NOT JUST THE PILOT!

Here we have air traffic control.
Tracking aircraft is their role.
Lining airplanes up in place,

making sure each one has space.
Scanning radar screens for blips,
they manage many sky-high trips.

Vehicles have jobs to do.
To cruise along they need a crew—

folks who make the transit run,
keep it safe for everyone.
Manage, mend, restore, improve . . .

Author's Note

Bus drivers, truckers, subway operators, train engineers, ferry captains, and airplane pilots have important jobs helping people and goods travel. But they are not the only ones who make vehicles go! All these helpers work on a team.

Next time you go for a ride, take a look around. Can you find people who are selling tickets, checking luggage, giving maps and directions, or collecting tolls? Do you see anyone repairing vehicles, the roads and tracks they travel on, or the lights and signals that keep us safe? Are the vehicles you ride and places you wait nice and clean? People worked hard to make everything sparkle!

Would you like to work on a team that makes transportation go? Which important job would *you* choose?

To Chambrae, Hilary, Katie, and Tracy—
I couldn't navigate these roads without you
—S. H. A.

For my son Izzy
—R. N.

BEACH LANE BOOKS · An imprint of Simon & Schuster Children's Publishing Division · 1230 Avenue of the Americas, New York, New York 10020 · Text © 2024 by Sara Holly Ackerman · Illustration © 2024 by Robert Neubecker · Book design © 2024 by Simon & Schuster, Inc. · All rights reserved, including the right of reproduction in whole or in part in any form. · BEACH LANE BOOKS and colophon are trademarks of Simon & Schuster, Inc. · Simon & Schuster: Celebrating 100 Years of Publishing in 2024 · For information about special discounts for bulk purchases, please contact Simon & Schuster Special Sales at 1-866-506-1949 or business@simonandschuster.com. · The Simon & Schuster Speakers Bureau can bring authors to your live event. For more information or to book an event, contact the Simon & Schuster Speakers Bureau at 1-866-248-3049 or visit our website at www.simonspeakers.com. · The text for this book was set in Vulpa. · The illustrations for this book were rendered digitally. · Manufactured in China · 1223 SCP · First Edition · 10 9 8 7 6 5 4 3 2 1 · Library of Congress Cataloging-in-Publication Data · Names: Ackerman, Sara Holly, author. | Neubecker, Robert, illustrator. · Title: Not just the driver! / Sara Holly Ackerman ; illustrated by Robert Neubecker. · Description: First edition. | New York : Beach Lane Books, [2024] | Audience: Ages 4–8 | Audience: Grades 2–3 | Summary: "Who makes buses and trains and boats and planes go? It's not just the driver! This rhyming read-aloud book celebrates all of the people who work behind the scenes to keep us moving, and introduces young readers to a whole slew of fun, and essential, transportation professions"— Provided by publisher. · Identifiers: LCCN 2023006529 (print) | LCCN 2023006530 (ebook) | ISBN 9781665936378 (hardcover) | ISBN 9781665936385 (ebook) · Subjects: LCSH: Transport workers—Juvenile literature. · Classification: LCC HD8039.T7 A37 2024 (print) | LCC HD8039.T7 (ebook) | DDC 388—dc23/eng/20230525 · LC record available at https://lccn.loc.gov/2023006529 · LC ebook record available at https://lccn.loc.gov/2023006530